DARK HUNTER

THE SIRENS' FEAST

Bloomsbury Education
An imprint of Bloomsbury Publishing Plc

50 Bedford Square
London
WC1B 3DP
UK

1385 Broadway
New York
NY 10018
USA

www.bloomsbury.com

Bloomsbury is a registered trade mark of Bloomsbury Publishing Plc

First published 2015

British Library Cataloguing-in-Publication Data
A catalogue record for this book is available from the British Library.

ISBN
PB: 978-1-4729-0828-5
ePub: 978-1-4729-0829-2
ePDF: 978-1-4729-0830-8
XML: 978-1-4729-2789-7

Library of Congress Cataloging-in-Publication Data
A catalog record for this book is available from the Library of Congress.

10 9 8 7 6 5 4 3 2 1

Typeset by Newgen Knowledge Works (P) Ltd., Chennai, India
Printed and bound by CPI Group (UK) Ltd, Croydon CR0 4YY

This book is produced using paper that is made from wood
grown in managed, sustainable forests. It is natural, renewable and
recyclable. The logging and manufacturing processes conform to the
environmental regulations of the country of origin.

To view more of our titles please visit www.bloomsbury.com

recommended by
CatchUp®
www.catchup.org

Catch Up is a not-for-profit charity
which aims to address the problem of
underachievement that has its roots in
literacy and numeracy difficulties.

DARK HUNTER

THE SIRENS' FEAST

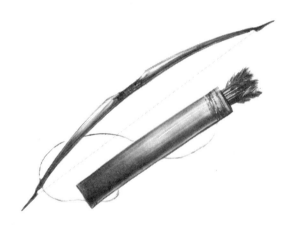

BENJAMIN HULME-CROSS

ILLUSTRATED BY NELSON EVERGREEN

A & C BLACK
AN IMPRINT OF BLOOMSBURY
LONDON NEW DELHI NEW YORK SYDNEY

The Dark Hunter

Mr Daniel Blood is the Dark Hunter.
People call him to fight evil demons,
vampires and ghosts.

Edgar and Mary help Mr Blood
with his work.

The three hunters need to be strong and
clever to survive…

Contents

Chapter 1

A Summer Meeting

Mr Blood, Mary and Edgar were high on a hill. They could see for miles all around. It was summer, and the sun was hot. But they could see storm clouds were coming towards them.

"We must find somewhere to stay tonight," said Mr Blood. He led the way down into a valley. The fields on either side of the path were just brown earth.

Edgar was surprised. "It's summer," he said. "The crops should be ready for harvest. But look, everything is dead." He was right. The crops had failed.

"Someone is coming," said Mary. A skinny boy was running towards them across the field.

"Do you have any food?" begged the boy. "We haven't eaten for days."

"Take this," said Mr Blood, handing over an apple and a loaf of bread from his pack. The boy put the bread under his arm and ran back across the field, eating the apple as he went.

They saw more empty fields and then came to a small village. More hungry people came to beg for food, just as the boy had done.

"We shouldn't stay here," Edgar whispered.

"You're right," said Mr Blood, "we haven't enough to feed them all and they could get nasty."

They handed over all the food they could spare and kept walking. Everywhere they looked the crops had failed.

"Poor people," Mr Blood said, shaking his head.

They came round a bend in the lane and saw a young woman. She was dressed all in white. She was humming softly to herself. As soon as Edgar and Mr Blood saw the woman they stopped and stared at her. They could not stop staring at her.

Mary spoke to the young woman. "Could you help us?" she asked. "There's a storm coming and we need somewhere to stay for the night."

"You can stay at my father's farm if you like," the young woman said. "We let guests stay with us all the time. Some of them stay for a long time." As she said this, she gave a strange smile.

Edgar and Mr Blood stood still, staring at the woman.

"Sorry about them," said Mary. "The boy is called Edgar, the man's name is Mr Blood and I'm Mary."

"Follow me," said the woman, turning away.

Mr Blood and Edgar both blinked and shook their heads. It was as if they had been in a dream and had just woken up.

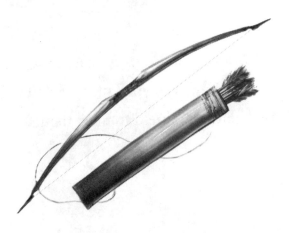

Chapter 2

The Farm

The young woman led them across a field towards a large farmhouse. A big man stood next to the house.

"Have you found some more guests for us?" he shouted. The woman in white nodded. The man seemed pleased and he hurried across the field to meet them.

"You must stay with us until the storm has passed," he said. "You have met my daughter, June. Now come inside and meet her sisters and my wife."

Mary saw that the farmer was carrying a bow.

The farmhouse door opened and a fat woman with red cheeks waved to them.

"Welcome, welcome!" she said, and then turned round to shout back through the door. "Lily! Rose! Come and meet our guests."

Two young women came out of the house. They both looked just like June. Mr Blood and Edgar stopped still, staring at them.

"Stop staring!" whispered Mary to Edgar. 'Remember your manners!"

"Triplets!" said the farmer, pointing at his three daughters. "I am a lucky man, aren't I?"

Mary was puzzled. She was thinking about the poor, starving boy who had asked them for food. And the villagers had been starving too. Yet the farmer and his wife were fat, and their daughters looked well-fed.

Mary wanted to ask Mr Blood what he thought. But when she looked at him, she saw that his eyes were blank. It was as if the three young women had put a spell on him and Edgar. Mary began to feel afraid.

They went into the farmhouse and sat down in the kitchen.

"I have some stew ready and you're welcome to eat with us," said the farmer's wife. "And we have plenty of beds in the house. You must stay until the storm has passed. Or stay longer," she added with a smile.

Mary remembered that June had said that, too. *"Some of them stay for a long time."* It felt like a threat to Mary now.

Mr Blood and Edgar ate the stew but Mary was afraid. She ate a few bites of the stew but that was all. She had no idea what was going on at the farm, but something felt wrong.

As soon as Edgar and Mr Blood had eaten all their food they both began to yawn. Mary pretended she was tired and she yawned too.

"You must be tired," said the farmer's wife. June will show you to the guest rooms so you can rest your tired legs."

June smiled sweetly, and started humming again. She led them upstairs and into three rooms. As soon as June left them, Mary crept out of her room and went to see Edgar. He was asleep on his bed, snoring. Mr Blood was asleep in his room too.

Mary knew something was very wrong. But she felt tired too. She had to lie down. She crept back to her room, lay down on the bed, and went to sleep.

Chapter 3

Sweet Music

When Mary woke she could hear the sweetest music she had ever heard. She lay on her back and listened to the music.

"I wonder if the storm is over?" she thought. And then she remembered the strange family, and how afraid she had felt.

Mary still felt very tired but she knew she must not go back to sleep. She stood up and went over to the window. The sky outside was pitch black. It had stopped raining.

Mary could still hear the music. It was someone singing.

It seemed to be coming from a barn close to the farmhouse. Mary could see that there was light inside the barn. She wanted to go and listen to the singing. She could not think about anything else.

Mary walked out of her room. On her way to the stairs, she looked into Edgar's room. His bed was empty. Mary checked on Mr Blood. His bed was empty too.

She crept downstairs. The farmer's bow and some arrows were leaning against a wall. She picked them up and opened the farmhouse door.

The singing was louder and Mary had
to fight to resist it. She put the bow and
arrows under her arm. Then she put her
hands over her ears to block the music out,
and crept towards the barn.

She walked around to the side of the barn and saw a small slit in the wall. It was too high up for her to see through. She looked around and saw a wooden box.

The box looked strong enough for Mary to stand on. She put down the bow and arrows to lift the box.

But when she took her hands away from her ears, the singing was too loud to resist. It felt as though the sound was pulling her towards the barn door.

"I need to block out the music!" thought Mary. She looked around for something that she could use. At last she saw some sheep's wool on the ground. She rolled up two small balls of wool and stuffed them into her ears.

Mary pushed the box over to the wall of the barn and climbed onto it. She looked through the slit in the wall, and gasped with horror.

Chapter 4

The Barn

Mr Blood and Edgar were standing still. Their eyes were open but they seemed to be in a deep sleep. June and her two sisters faced them. They were singing.

On the other side of the barn, Mary saw the farmer and his wife. They both wore aprons. In their hands they held big, sharp knives.

Mary felt the horror rise inside her. She cried out, and the farmer and his wife looked up. The sisters kept singing. Mr Blood and Edgar didn't move. The farmer gave a wicked smile.

Mary jumped off the box and ran to the barn door. She shoved it. She kicked it. But she couldn't open it. The only way she could save Edgar and Mr Blood was to stop the sisters singing.

Mary raced back to the box, and grabbed the bow and arrows. She climbed up again, and took aim through the slit in the wall. She fired.

The arrow flew through the air and hit one of the sisters. The young woman fell to the ground. Her two sisters stopped singing.

Mr Blood and Edgar blinked and shook their heads. It was as if they were waking up from a deep sleep. They saw the farmer with his knives coming towards them.

Mr Blood and Edgar ran towards the door but the farmer was too quick for them. He reached the door first and blocked their way.

Mary knew it was up to her to save their lives. She put another arrow in the bow. Her arm was trembling as she took aim. The arrow flew through the air and hit the farmer in the arm. He howled with rage and ran towards Edgar, holding a knife above his head.

At last, Mr Blood managed to unbolt the door. He and Edgar ran out into the night. They slammed the door shut behind them and leaned against it.

Mary raced around to meet them and picked up a wooden post that was leaning against the wall. She slid it across the door to bolt it from the outside.

The farmer crashed against the door. He threw himself against it over and over again. But the door held firm.

Mr Blood, Mary and Edgar looked at one another.

"The farmer's daughters are Sirens," said Mr Blood. "They bewitch people with their singing and then kill them. Mary, you have done very, very well. Without you, Edgar and I would be dead."

They could hear the farmer screaming with rage inside the barn.

"What do we do now?" said Edgar.

"They have to be destroyed," said Mr Blood. "They are monsters. They eat human flesh."

"So that is why they look so well when everyone else in the area is starving," said Edgar.

"How can we stop them?" asked Mary.

Mr Blood led Mary and Edgar back to the farmhouse. A fire was still burning in the grate. Mr Blood held one of the arrows in the flames until it caught fire.

"Give me the bow," said Mr Blood. He sounded grim. Mary handed him the bow and they went outside.

Mr Blood took aim. He shot the burning arrow into the straw roof of the barn. Quickly the straw began to burn.

Mary looked shocked. "Is there no other way?" she asked Mr Blood.

Mr Blood shook his head. "Those animals are not humans," he said. "They will go on killing people and eating their flesh if we don't stop it now."

"Mr Blood is right," said Edgar. "It is for the best."

And the three of them turned and walked away.